Big Hugs, Little Hugs

Big Hugs, Little Hugs

Felicia Bond

Philomel Books

An Imprint of Penguin Group (USA) Inc.

Everyone hugs all
over the world.

Cats hug

Dogs hug

Bears hug

Hogs hug

Hamsters hug

Hippos hug

On this side

And that side

Upstairs

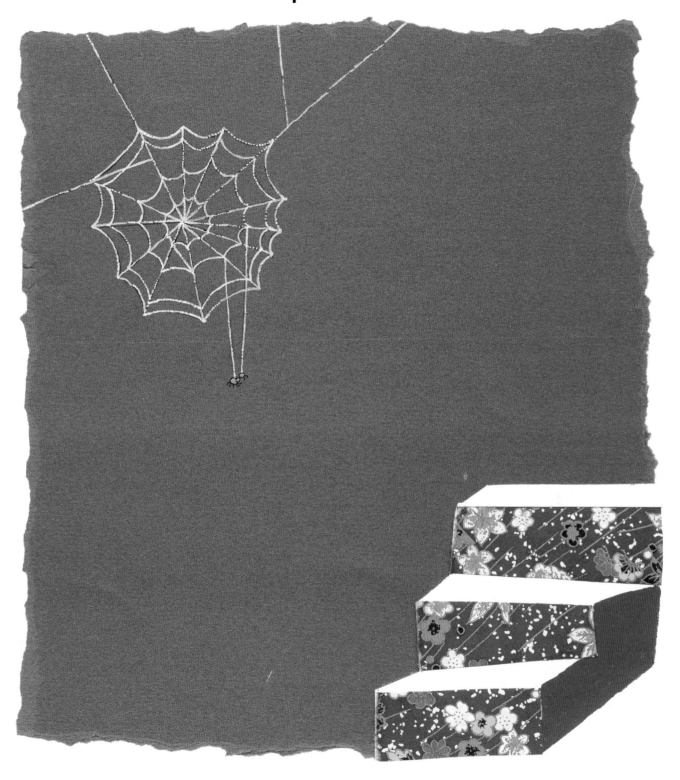

Downstairs

Inside

Outside

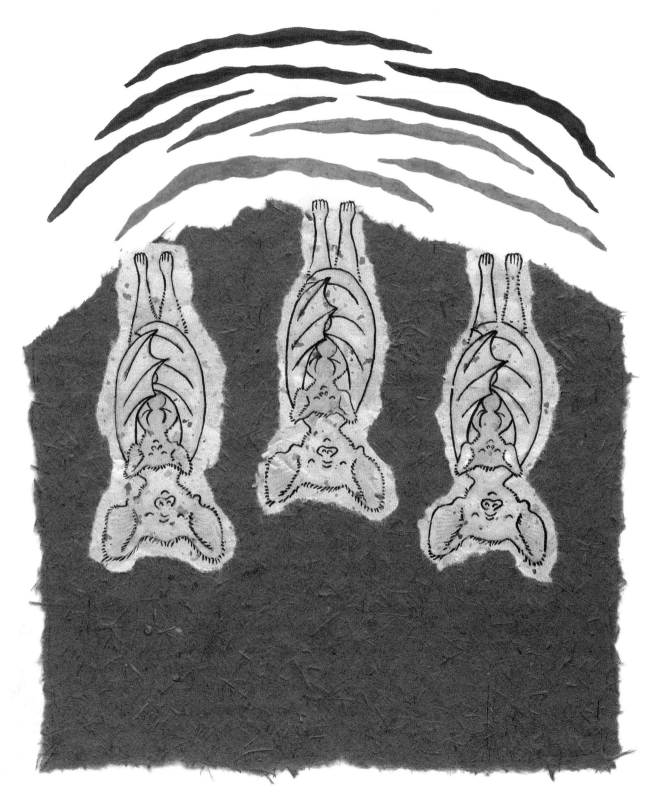

Here

And there

Big hugs

Little hugs

In winter

And summer

Day

And night

In the past

And in the future

Everyone hugs

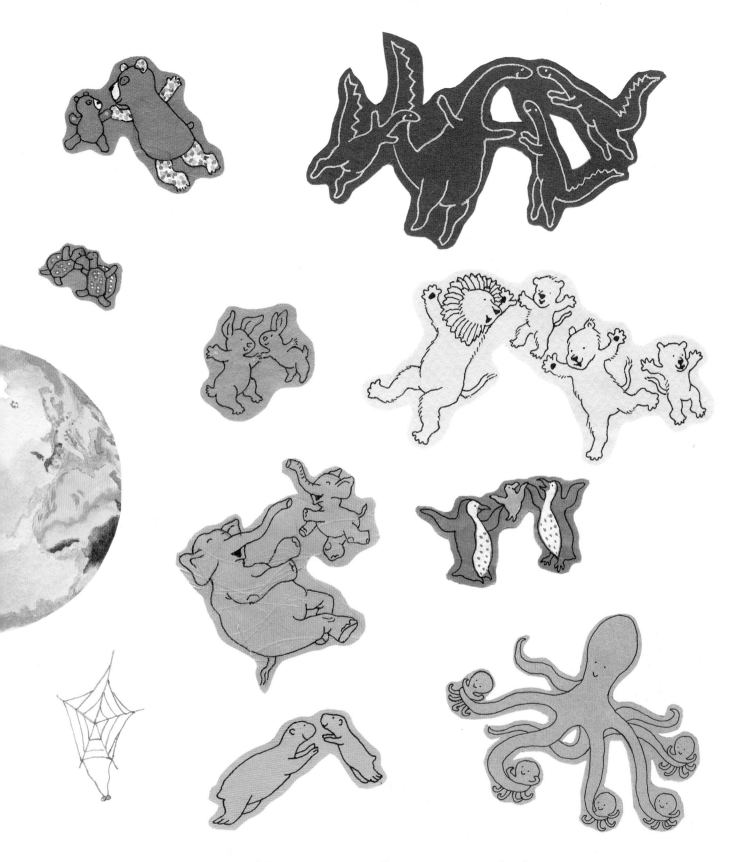

All over the world.

PHILOMEL BOOKS

A division of Penguin Young Readers Group. Published by The Penguin Group.
Penguin Group (USA) Inc., 375 Hudson Street, New York, NY 10014, U.S.A.
Penguin Group (Canada), 90 Eglinton Avenue East, Suite 700, Toronto, Ontario M4P 2Y3, Canada (a division of Pearson Penguin Canada Inc.).
Penguin Books Ltd, 80 Strand, London WC2R 0RL, England.
Penguin Ireland, 25 St. Stephen's Green, Dublin 2, Ireland (a division of Penguin Books Ltd).
Penguin Group (Australia), 250 Camberwell Road, Camberwell, Victoria 3124, Australia (a division of Pearson Australia Group Pty Ltd).
Penguin Books India Pvt Ltd, 11 Community Centre, Panchsheel Park, New Delhi - 110 017, India.
Penguin Group (NZ), 67 Apollo Drive, Rosedale, Auckland 0632, New Zealand (a division of Pearson New Zealand Ltd).
Penguin Books (South Africa) (Pty) Ltd, 24 Sturdee Avenue, Rosebank, Johannesburg 2196, South Africa.
Penguin Books Ltd, Registered Offices: 80 Strand, London WC2R 0RL, England.

Design by Semadar Megged.   Edited by Jill Santopolo.   Text set in 31-point Legacy Sans ITC.

Library of Congress Cataloging-in-Publication Data
Bond, Felicia.   Big hugs, little hugs / Felicia Bond.—1st ed.   p. cm.   Summary: Illustrations and brief text show many different ways to hug.
[1. Hugging—Fiction.] I. Title. PZ7.B63666Bi 2012 [E]—dc22 2010053139
ISBN 978-0-399-25614-1
3 5 7 9 10 8 6 4 2